DOG'S
NOISY DAY

Copyright © 2002 by Tucker Slingsby Ltd
All rights reserved.
Devised and produced by Tucker Slingsby Ltd
Roebuck House, 288 Upper Richmond Road West, London, SW14 7JG

CIP Data is available.

Published in the United States 2003 by Dutton Children's Books,
a division of Penguin Putnam Books for Young Readers
345 Hudson Street, New York, New York 10014
www.penguinputnam.com
Printed in Singapore • First American Edition
ISBN 0-525-47015-8
2 4 6 8 10 9 7 5 3 1

DOG'S NOISY DAY

A Story to Read Aloud

Emma Dodd

Dutton Children's Books

New York

Dog is just waking up.
Hello, Dog!
He makes his morning noise.

YAWN!

Outside, a bird makes her
morning noise.
It's prettier than Dog's noise.

Cat **MEOWS** to Dog
on his way outside.
Dog is too hungry
to play chase.
GRRRR! says his stomach.

**After breakfast,
Dog is ready for adventure.**

With the wind in his ears,
he scampers along to find some.

"COCK-A-DOODLE-DOO!"
A rooster crows to wake up
the neighboring farm.
It certainly works on Dog!

Dog tries to crow like the rooster.
"WOOFA, WOOFLE, WOO!"

The cows laugh.
"MOO MOO MOO!
Good morning to you!"

An even better noise is coming
from the bushes.
Dog scrambles through
to investigate.

"HEE-HAW, HEE-HAW!"
A donkey is laughing, too.
This is a friendly farm, thinks Dog.

In the field, Dog sees
some little houses.
Doghouses! thinks Dog.
New friends!

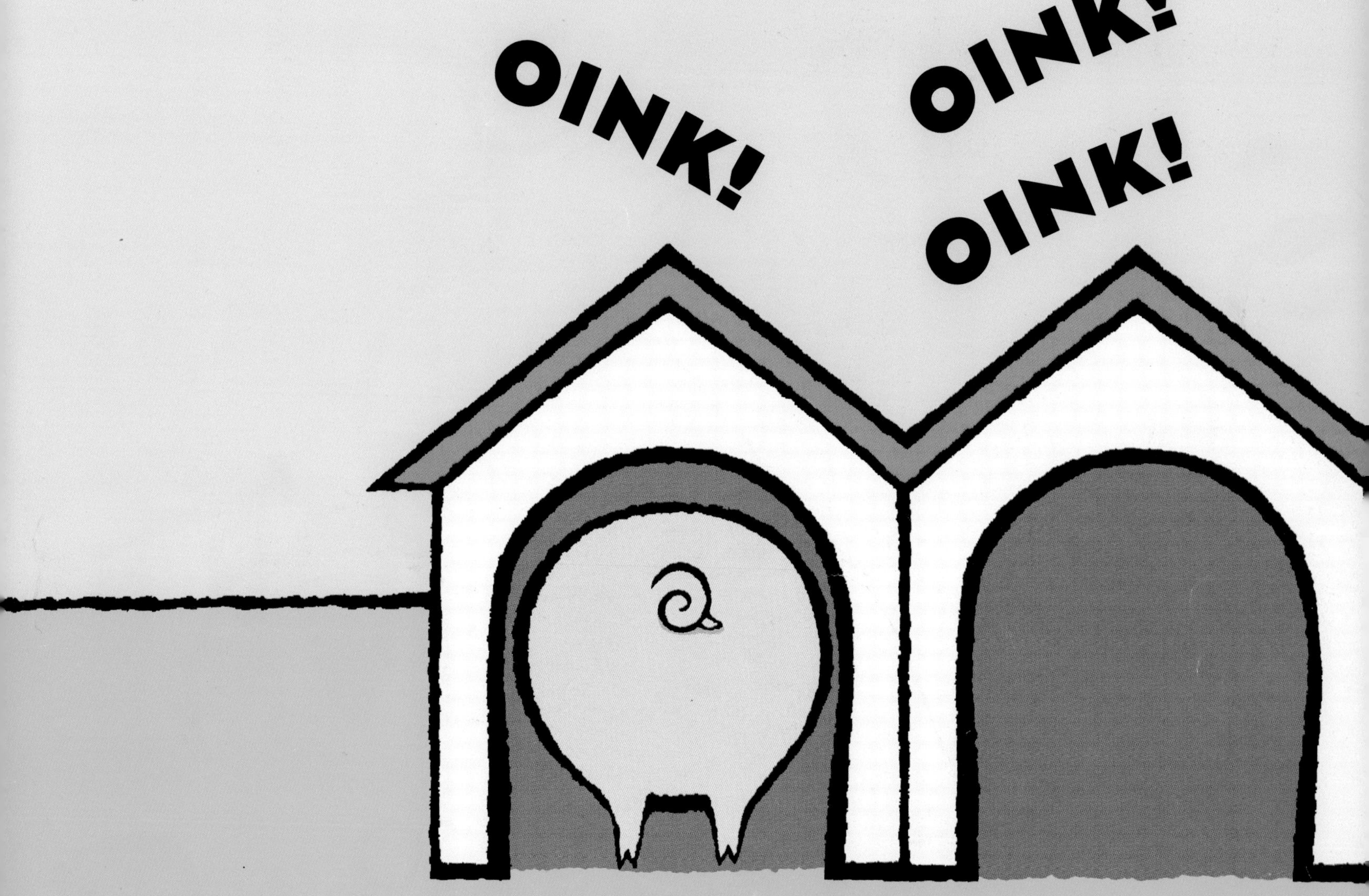
OINK!
OINK!
OINK!

Dog doesn't find other dogs,
but he does find friends and
some messy fun.
SLURP! goes the mud.
"OINK! OINK!" say the piglets.

OINK! OINK!

Dog needs a bath. The ducks QUACK and the geese HONK as Dog dives into their pond.

Clean and dry, Dog curls up for a rest. Bumblebees make soft, **BUZZ**ing noises that lull Dog to sleep.

BUZZ

The sun is sinking in the sky.
"TWIT-A-WOO!"
The owl's nighttime noise
lets Dog know that it's
time to go home.

TWIT-A-WOO!

Dog's friends say good-bye.